The Race for
Gold Rush Treasure:
California (USA)

4

THE SECRET AGENTS
JACK AND MAX STALWART SERIES

Book 1—The Battle for the Emerald Buddha **(Thailand)**

Book 2—The Adventure in the Amazon **(Brazil)**

Book 3—The Fate of the Irish Treasure **(Ireland)**

Book 4—The Race for Gold Rush Treasure **California (USA)**

THE SECRET AGENT
JACK STALWART SERIES

Book 1—The Escape of the Deadly Dinosaur **New York (USA)**

Book 2—The Search for the Sunken Treasure **(Australia)**

Book 3—The Mystery of the Mona Lisa **(France)**

Book 4—The Caper of the Crown Jewels **(England)**

Book 5—The Secret of the Sacred Temple **(Cambodia)**

Book 6—The Pursuit of the Ivory Poachers **(Kenya)**

Book 7—The Puzzle of the Missing Panda **(China)**

Book 8—Peril at the Grand Prix **(Italy)**

Book 9—The Deadly Race to Space **(Russia)**

Book 10—The Quest for Aztec Gold **(Mexico)**

Book 11—The Theft of the Samurai Sword **(Japan)**

Book 12—The Fight for the Frozen Land **(Arctic)**

Book 13—The Hunt for the Yeti Skull **(Nepal)**

Book 14—The Mission to Find Max **(Egypt)**

For more information visit
www.elizabethsingerhunt.com

The Race for
Gold Rush Treasure:
California (USA)

Elizabeth Singer Hunt
Illustrated by Brian Williamson

RP|KIDS
PHILADELPHIA

Running Press Kids
Hachette Book Group
1290 Avenue of the Americas, New York, NY 10104
www.runningpress.com/rpkids
@RP_Kids

Printed in the United States of America

First Edition: March 2019

Published by Running Press Kids, an imprint of Perseus Books, LLC, a subsidiary of Hachette Book Group, Inc. The Running Press Kids name and logo is a trademark of the Hachette Book Group.

The Hachette Speakers Bureau provides a wide range of authors for speaking events. To find out more, go to www.hachettespeakersbureau.com or call (866) 376-6591.

The publisher is not responsible for websites (or their content) that are not owned by the publisher.

Photograph of James Marshall, discoverer of gold, at Sutter's Mill from the Library of Congress, LC-USZ62-137164 DLC (b&w film copy neg.)

Print book cover and interior design by Jason Kayser and Rachel Peckman.

Library of Congress Control Number: 2017963211

ISBNs: 978-1-6028-6579-2 (paperback), 978-1-6028-6580-8 (ebook)

LSC-C

10 9 8 7 6 5 4 3 2 1

For Callie. Woof!

THE WORLD

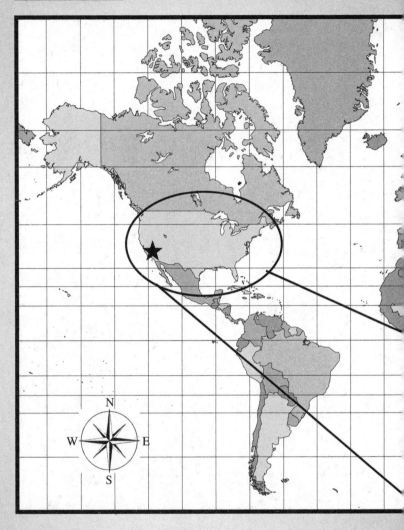

Destination:
CALIFORNIA (USA)

GLOBAL PROTECTION FORCE ALERT

THE WORLD'S MOST PRECIOUS TREASURES ARE UNDER ATTACK!

Secret Agents Courage and Wisdom recently thwarted an attempt to steal the *Emerald Buddha* from the Grand Palace in Thailand. The GPF believes that the mastermind behind this crime was also behind the thefts of Picasso's *Acrobat* painting and a Fabergé egg from Russia. If this is true, we have a madman on our hands.

GLOBAL PROTECTION FORCE ALERT

All agents must be prepared to travel at a moment's notice. Anyone witnessing someone or something suspicious should report it immediately to Gerald Barter, the Director of the GPF.

Louise Persnall

Louise Persnall
Assistant to Gerald Barter

THINGS YOU'LL FIND IN EVERY BOOK

Global Protection Force (GPF): The GPF is a worldwide force of junior secret agents whose aim is to protect the world's people, places, and possessions. It was started in 1947 by a man named Ronald Barter, who wanted to stop criminals from harming things that mattered in the world. When Ronald died, under mysterious circumstances, his son Gerald took over. The GPF's main offices are located somewhere in the Arctic Circle.

Watch Phone: The GPF's Watch Phone is worn by GPF agents around their wrists. It can make and receive phone calls, send and receive messages, play videos, unlock the Secret Agent Book Bag, and track an agent's whereabouts. The Watch Phone also carries the GPF's Melting Ink Pen. Just push the button to the left of the screen to eject this lifesaving gadget.

Secret Agent Book Bag: The GPF's Secret Agent Book Bag is licensed only to GPF agents. Inside are hi-tech gadgets necessary to foil bad guys and escape certain death. To unlock and lock, all an agent has to do is place his or her thumb on the zipper. The automatic thumbprint reader will identify him or her as the owner.

GPF Tablet: The GPF Tablet is a tablet computer used by GPF agents at home. On it, agents can access the GPF secure website, send encrypted e-mails, use the agent directory, and download mission-critical data.

Whizzy: Whizzy is Jack's magical miniature globe. Almost every night at 7:30 p.m., the GPF uses him to send Jack the location of his next mission. Jack's parents don't know that Whizzy is anything but an ordinary globe. Jack's brother, Max, has a similar buddy on his bedside table named "Zoom."

The Magic Map: The Magic Map is a world map that hangs on every GPF agent's wall. Recently, it was upgraded from wood to a hi-tech, unbreakable glass. Once an agent places the country shape in the right spot, the map lights up and transports him or her to his or her mission. The agent returns precisely one minute after he or she left.

DESTINATION: CALIFORNIA

CALIFORNIA

California is known as the "Golden State." Gold was discovered here in 1848. Its state flower is the golden poppy.

California became the thirty-first state in the United States of America on September 9, 1850.

There are more people living in California than any other state. Nearly 40 million people live there.

The Golden Gate Bridge, one of the world's most famous bridges, is located in San Francisco, California. It's painted orange so that people can see it through the fog.

The largest living tree on the planet, a sequoia nicknamed "General Sherman," lives in California. It may also be one of the oldest. Some think it could be 2,700 years old.

Death Valley, the hottest place in North America, is in the southern part of the state. The hottest temperature ever recorded was 134°F (in 1913).

California is home to the lowest and highest points in the continental United States. Badwater Basin in Death Valley is 282 feet below sea level. Mt. Whitney soars 14,494 feet above.

The first Disneyland opened in 1955 in Anaheim, California. It was created by Walt Disney, the genius behind *Cinderella*, *Mary Poppins*, and *Snow White and the Seven Dwarfs*.

California is an agricultural state. It grows many things including grapes, olives, garlic, lemons, avocados, almonds, strawberries, and broccoli.

Black bears, mountain lions, bobcats, bald eagles, quail, and diamondback rattlesnakes call California home. Whales, sea lions, and dolphins swim off its coast.

HISTORY OF THE CALIFORNIA GOLD RUSH

James Marshall in front of Sutter's Mill in Coloma, California.

On January 24, 1848, James Marshall discovered gold in Coloma, California. He found it near a sawmill he was building next to the American River. He and his boss, John Sutter, tried to keep their discovery a secret.

In 1849, word got out. Hundreds of thousands of people (mostly men) from around the world moved to the area to strike it rich.

Some came from faraway places like China. Others traveled

across America by horse and by foot. The journey was filled with danger.

Travelers met with disease, starvation, dehydration, poisonous reptiles, bad weather, and accidents. It could take up to seven months just to get to California's gold country. Sadly, many men, women, and children died along the way.

Once there, miners had to work hard to find gold. Many "panned" for it by standing in the river and swirling gravel, dirt, and water around in a steel pan.

If they were lucky, gold flakes or nuggets would settle to the bottom.

The people who sold equipment and supplies to the desperate miners were the ones that made reliable money.

At least 100,000 Native Americans died during the California Gold Rush. Greedy miners killed them for their land and gave them deadly diseases.

By 1852, "easy-to-find" gold was hard to find. The California Gold Rush ended in 1855.

GOLD MINER'S TOOL KIT

Pick axe
(to break down rock)

Knife
(to pick gold
out of rocks)

Steel pan
(to pan for gold)

Gun
(to protect yourself
and your claim)

Shovel
(to dig gravel
and dirt)

Bucket
(to carry debris
or water)

GOLD 101

Gold is a precious metal. Its chemical symbol is **Au**.

✦

Pure gold has a yellow, slightly reddish hue.

✦

Gold is thought to have been created from the collision of collapsed stars billions of years ago.

✦

Gold is extremely heavy and dense. It's denser than lead and nineteen times denser than water. That's why gold sinks to the bottom.

Although it's heavy, gold is soft. This means it can be easily spread and shaped.

✦

Gold can be beaten into extremely thin sheets. It's also used in jewelry.

✦

Gold is worth more than $1,000 per troy ounce.

THE STALWART FAMILY

Jack Stalwart: Nine-year-old Jack Stalwart works as a secret agent for the Global Protection Force, or GPF. Jack originally joined the GPF to find and rescue his brother, Max, who'd disappeared on one of his missions. Eventually, Jack tracked Max to Egypt, where he saved him *and* King Tut's diadem, or crown.

Max Stalwart: Twelve-year-old Max is a GPF agent too. He was recruited after

filling out a questionnaire online, and pledging his young life to protect "that which cannot protect itself." Max's specialty within the GPF is cryptography, which is the ability to write and crack coded messages. Recently, Max narrowly escaped death in Egypt, while protecting King Tut's diadem.

John Stalwart: John Stalwart is the patriarch of the family. He's an aerospace engineer, who recently headed up the Mars Mission Program. For many months, the GPF had fooled John and his wife, Corinne, into thinking that their oldest son, Max, was at a boarding school in Switzerland. Really, Max was on a top secret mission in Egypt. When that mission ended, Max's "boarding school" closed, and he returned home for good. John is an American and his wife, Corinne, is British, which makes Jack and Max a bit of both.

Corinne Stalwart: Corinne Stalwart is the family matriarch. She's kind, loving, and fair. She's also totally unaware (as is her husband) that her two sons are agents for the Global Protection Force. In her spare time, Corinne volunteers at the boys' school, and studies Asian art.

GPF GADGET INSTRUCTION MANUAL

Spy Scope: The GPF's Spy Scope is the perfect gadget for spying on criminals without them knowing. Its flexible black wire can bend to reach around corners, under doors, and through small keyholes. Mounted on the top is a hidden camera that syncs directly with the screen on a Watch Phone.

Diversion Safe: When you need to hide your top secret items in plain sight, use one of the GPF's Diversion Safes. The GPF's Diversion Safe is a realistic-looking object with a hidden compartment inside. Agents can choose from a number of options including a clock, book, hairbrush, soda can, flowerpot, water bottle, and rock. An agent can also make his or her own. Just follow the instructions found in the *GPF's Secret Agent Training Manual.*

GPF Kayak: The GPF Kayak is the world's smallest portable kayak. Just open this square packet and watch as the boat instantly unfolds into shape. The GPF Kayak fits one person weighing no more than 175 pounds. Make sure to pair it with the GPF Oar. (See below.)

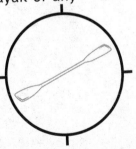

GPF Oar: The GPF Oar is a portable paddle that pairs with the GPF Kayak or any watercraft available. Just pull three times on this short tube and watch as the shaft expands in length. Uncapping the top end of the tube releases a blade made of flexible plastic, which hardens as soon as it touches the air.

Chapter 1
The Coded Letter

In a filthy Mexican jail cell, a prisoner
sat on his bed holding a letter that he'd
received that day. The note was written
in childlike handwriting. There were
twelve pink pony stickers scattered
across the page. Anyone who looked at
the note would think it was written by a
little girl. But the prisoner knew better.
It was a message from a member of his
adult gang.

He pulled the first sticker off the page.
The word "MEET" was written on the
page underneath. Under the second
sticker was the word "AT." The third
sticker revealed the time "11:30 p.m."

After removing the rest of the stickers,
the man studied the message.

*Meet at 11:30 p.m. tonight. Gas station
5 miles due west. Gold awaits.*

The prisoner grunted with pleasure.

BANG!

The door to the cellblock clanged open against the wall behind it. A skinny prison guard sporting a handlebar mustache entered the cellblock. He walked down the hallway and checked in on each of the ten prisoners. The inmate stuffed the note into this trouser pocket before the guard arrived at his cell.

"Lights out in five minutes!" shouted the guard in Spanish.

The prisoner nodded to the man. He'd already been in the prison for sixty days. He knew the schedule. At 10 p.m. every night, the lights went out. Most of the prisoners used the time to sleep. But not this prisoner. He used the nighttime hours to prepare his escape.

As soon as he'd arrived, the man had stolen a spoon from the prison cafeteria. Every night since, he'd used it to scrape at the soft wall near the floor of his cell. Just last week, he'd managed to make a hole big enough to fit through. Now that his gang was ready for him, all the prisoner had to do was escape.

CLICK.

The lights went out.

The prisoner waited for the other inmates to fall asleep. Then he moved the bedside table that was covering the hole to the side. He got down on his hands and knees and slithered through it. Once outside, he began to run.

In front of him was a tall barbed wire fence. A spotlight from above was zigzagging across the grounds. He waited

for the light to move somewhere else,
then he bolted for the fence.

He climbed it and thrust his body over
the barbs. They ripped at his clothes
and sliced into his skin. But the prisoner
didn't care. He was Callous Carl, the
toughest treasure hunter on the planet.
As soon as his feet hit the ground, he ran
across the Mexican desert and toward the
lights of the gas station ahead.

Chapter 2
The Golden Discovery

Nine-year-old Jack Stalwart was sitting at the kitchen table reading the latest issue of *Archaeology Kids*. *Archaeology Kids* or *"AK"* was a weekly magazine dedicated to stories of archaeological discovery around the world.

Archaeology was the study of history through the excavation of ancient places and objects. An archaeologist was the person who did the excavation. Not only

were the magazine's articles interesting, they were also necessary for Jack's job.

Jack and his brother, Max, were secret agents for the Global Protection Force, or GPF. Their mission was to protect the world's most precious people, places, and possessions. Nearly every night at 7:30 p.m., they were sent on dangerous adventures around the globe.

One of the stories in the magazine caught Jack's attention.

EUREKA! GOLD DISCOVERED AGAIN IN CALIFORNIA!

An archaeologist has discovered a strongbox containing rare gold coins and nuggets from the California Gold Rush. Its estimated value is $25 million. The area where the box was found is less than ten miles from where gold was first discovered in 1848.

During that year, a worker named James Marshall discovered gold in the American River. He and his boss, John Sutter, decided to keep the discovery a secret. But in 1849, word got out and hundreds of thousands of people flocked to the area. This period in American history is known as the "California Gold Rush." The people who came to strike it rich were known as the "49ers."

The recent discovery of the gold is personal for the dig's archaeologist, Mary Sutter. Mary is a distant relative of John Sutter, the man who owned the mill where the gold was found in 1848. Mary is currently cataloging the find and hopes to move the hoard to a more secure location within the week.

When asked for details about the treasure's location, Mary just smiled. "I can't tell you where it is," she said. "But I can tell you that we are working to protect it."

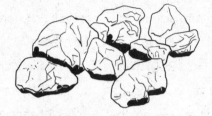

Chapter 3
The Breaking News

Just then, the kitchen door swung open. Jack's brother, Max, was standing in the doorway. Max had just returned from a pizza party celebrating the end of his soccer season. Max was the goalkeeper for the local team, the "Surrey Swarm."

"Did you hear?" asked Max.

Jack wasn't sure what his brother was talking about.

"Hear what?" asked Jack.

"Callous Carl's escaped," said Max.

Jack froze. He wasn't expecting his brother to say *that*.

Max pulled his GPF Tablet out of his bag. Recently, the GPF had upgraded it to include facial recognition software. Instead of using a password or thumbprint to sign in, all an agent had to do was look at it. Max lifted the tablet to his face and then handed it to Jack.

Jack read the information on the screen.

GPF NEWS FLASH

Notorious treasure hunter Callous Carl has escaped from a Mexican prison through a hole in his cell wall. A mangled spoon was discovered nearby.

Sniffer dogs have traced his scent to a gas station five miles west. Authorities think he was collected there by an accomplice driving a car. If you have any information about the whereabouts of this dangerous individual, please contact the GPF immediately.

Jack couldn't help but feel more than a bit nervous. After all, it was Jack who'd put Callous Carl in prison in the first place. He'd caught the treasure hunter

trying to steal Aztec gold in Mexico.
Before being taken away, Carl had
threatened Jack. "I'm going to get you,"
he said. Now that Callous Carl was out
of prison, there was no telling what he
would do next.

Max noticed the worried look on Jack's
face.

"Don't worry," said Max. "He's
thousands of miles away. Besides, Callous
Carl doesn't know anything about you. He
doesn't even know where you live."

Max was right. The only thing Callous
knew about Jack was what he looked like.
Fortunately, it had been two months since
he'd seen him. Besides, reasoned Jack,
Mexico was halfway around the globe.
The odds of running into the man were
"Slim to none, and Slim left town." At
least that's what Jack's aunt Sally from
Louisiana always used to say.

The good news for Jack was that there was no time to freak out. It was 7:27 p.m. There were more important things waiting for him in his room.

Chapter 4
The Portal

Jack and Max headed upstairs. At the top
of the steps, Max hung a left, while Jack
took a right. Before they entered their
individual bedrooms, the brothers winked
at each other.

Jack stepped into his room and closed
the door. The bookcase on his left
contained some of his favorite books.
There were the Hardy Boys Mysteries,
Swallows and Amazons, and Enid

Blyton's The Famous Five. There were also nonfiction titles like *Guinness World Records*, *World Atlas*, *How to Draw Cartoons*, and *The History of Rock Climbing*.

Next to Jack's bookcase was his desk. Above that was a corkboard with notes and photos from his friends. On the wall opposite Jack was none other than the

Magic Map. This was the portal through which the GPF sent Jack away on his missions. (Max had a similar Magic Map in his room too.) Next to that was Jack's animated globe, Whizzy. Whizzy was the device that gave Jack the location of his missions.

Scattered throughout Jack's room were several "Diversion Safes." A Diversion

Safe was a realistic-looking object with a hidden compartment inside. Instead of pages in the American history book on his shelf, there was a hollowed center. The tissue box on his desk was a Diversion Safe too. The bottom was missing, and there was no tissue inside. Jack was particularly proud of the last one, because he'd made it himself. Just as he was thinking about which Diversion Safe to make next, Jack's globe, Whizzy, woke up.

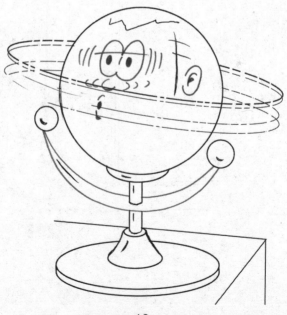

Whizzy began to spin furiously until he coughed—"Ahem!" A jigsaw piece in the shape of a country flew out of his mouth and hung in the air.

As soon as Jack saw it, he knew what it was. It was the United States of America.

On one of his previous missions, Jack had been sent to New York City. There, he'd been tasked with capturing a rampaging dinosaur. Jack wondered whether he'd be sent back to New York, or whether another part of America needed his help.

Jack used his hand to swipe the piece over to the Magic Map. As soon as he put it over the USA, the piece sunk in and a red light appeared.

He hurried to his bed and pulled his Book Bag out from underneath. After their failed mission in Ireland, both Jack and Max had to be issued new Watch

Phones and Book Bags. Jack checked to
make sure his gadgets were inside. Then
he strapped the bag to his back and
returned to the Magic Map.

As soon as the red light inside the
USA grew, Jack said, "Off to the USA!"
Then the light flickered and burst and
swallowed Jack into the Magic Map.

Chapter 5
The Golden Mission

When Jack arrived, he found himself in
the middle of a forest. But this wasn't
like the rain forest of Brazil. This one
was open and dry. Its green pine and fir
trees were spread apart and the grasses
on the hills were brown and parched.
Jack checked his Watch Phone for the
temperature outside. It was a toasty 90°F.

According to the topographical map
on his Watch Phone, Jack was fifty yards

south of where he needed to be. All
contacts had to give the GPF coordinates
of the mission meeting point. That way,
the GPF could program them into an
agent's Magic Map. The coordinates were
based on the longitude and latitude of
the earth.

Jack followed the directions through
a clump of trees. A striped chipmunk
scattered across his path. A woodpecker

tapped on a nearby tree. Lying on the ground were hundreds of brown pine needles.

Soon, the trees opened up into a small clearing.

Hanging from a tree at the edge was a rusty tin can. Just below that was a large square pit. The pit was about three feet deep. Surrounding the area was a white string staked at each of the four corners of the square. Small trowels and pickaxes were scattered throughout.

Inside the pit was a woman. She was kneeling and brushing at something in the ground. Figuring this was his contact, Jack made his way over. But out of nowhere, an animal attacked!

It charged at him from the right and pinned him to the ground. Panicked, Jack tried to think what kind of animal it could be. There were lots of predatory animals in the USA, including mountain lions and bears. But as soon as Jack saw what it was, he breathed a sigh of relief. It was a large brown dog.

The dog playfully jumped off of Jack and wagged its tail.

Woof!

Woof!

Woof!

Jack sat up on his elbows and looked

at the tag on the dog's collar. It said
"Callie."

"Hi, Callie," said Jack, brushing the dust
off of his trousers. "Nice to meet you."

Woof!

Woof!

Woof!

By now, the woman in the pit had
noticed Jack. She made her way over to
him. The woman was about fifty years old

with long, wavy brown hair. There was a notepad stuffed into the belt of her jeans. Dirt was on her knees from where she'd been kneeling.

"Sorry about that," she said. "Callie can sometimes get a bit *too* friendly."

"That's all right," said Jack. "I love dogs."

Jack loved dogs so much that he

even volunteered for the local animal shelter.

"I'm Mary Sutter," she said, sticking out her hand.

As Jack was shaking it, he realized something. He recognized that name. It was the name of the archaeologist that he'd read about in his *AK* magazine.

"Wow," said Jack, almost starstruck.

He'd never met a famous archaeologist before.

"The GPF said they'd be sending their finest," said Mary.

Jack didn't want to brag, but he *was* one of their most decorated agents.

"They already have," said a voice from behind the trees.

"Huh?" said Jack.

When Jack saw who it was, he rolled his eyes. Max walked over to Mary and Jack with a cheeky grin.

"Do you two know each other?" she asked.

"You could say that," said Max. "We're brothers."

"When I asked for a couple of agents," said Mary, "I had no idea they'd be sending brothers!"

"Neither did I," thought Jack.

He loved his brother. But he kind of

wanted this mission to himself. A fly
buzzed past Jack. He shooed it away.

"So what seems to be the problem?"
asked Max.

"There's no problem," said Mary.

Jack and Max looked confused.

"But I *do* need your help with
something," she said.

She led the boys over to the pit. Inside
was a rectangular box. Although most of
the box had been excavated, the bottom
was still stuck in the ground.

Mary opened the lid. When Jack and
Max saw what was inside, their eyes

opened wide. There were hundreds of gold coins and nuggets. Jack remembered the article in *AK*. It said the find was worth $25 million. The boys were speechless. They'd never seen this much gold in one place in their lives.

"It dates back to the California Gold Rush," she said.

Some of the coins were stamped with the year 1851. Others were marked with 1852. Jack knew that the California Gold Rush began in 1848 when James Marshall discovered gold in Coloma, California. For many years after that, people flocked to the area to strike it rich.

"This is called a 'strongbox,'" she explained. "Banks used them to carry gold coins and nuggets when they traveled by stagecoach."

"How did it end up here?" asked Max.

"Somebody probably stole it," said Mary, "and buried it here for a later date. But for whatever reason, they never came back."

"What do you need us to do?" asked Jack.

"As soon as I take it out of the ground," she explained, "I need to raft it downstream to the nearest town. From there, I have to drive it to San Francisco. There's an expert waiting to authenticate the coins."

"And you want us to provide protection?" asked Max.

Mary nodded.

"I'll have the box out of the ground within the hour," said Mary. "In the meantime, why don't the two of you head down to the river? Who knows, maybe you'll find some gold of your own."

Chapter 6
The Fool's Gold

Callie stayed behind with Mary. The boys
made their way to the American River,
which was a five-minute walk from the
camp. The American River was the place
where James Marshall found gold in 1848.
It was also where hundreds of thousands
of miners worked and lived to try and
make a fortune.

Jack gazed at the glistening river in
front of him. He watched as it rushed

over the rocks in its way. Jack wondered what life had been like for a 49er. He knew that the work was backbreaking and long.

Most of them spent their days in the freezing river, swirling gravel, dirt, and water around in pans. Sometimes, they'd find a flake of gold. Sometimes, they'd get a bigger nugget. Most of the time, they found absolutely nothing. By 1852, the "easy gold" was hard to find.

Jack plunged his hands into the water. He dug into the riverbed and scooped up some of the rocks. Flakes of bright yellow rose to the surface. He was shocked. He didn't think finding gold was going to be this easy.

"Eureka!" he cried.

Max looked over at the water and laughed.

"That's not real gold, you silly," said
Max. "That's *fool's* gold."

Jack had never heard of "fool's gold"
before.

"It's a mineral called 'pyrite,'" said Max.
"It looks like gold, but it isn't."

Jack wondered if the 49ers were
constantly being tricked by fool's
gold too.

   Disappointed, he pulled his hands
out of the water and wiped them on his
trousers. Another fly buzzed around Jack.
He shooed this one away too.

   Just then, they heard a tinkling sound
behind them. It was the sound of a
silver dog tag clinking against a collar.
It was Callie.

   Woof!

Woof!

She burst through the forest and onto the bank. Excitedly, she ran back and forth along the river. She splashed water all over Jack and Max.

"Callie!" said Jack and Max at the same time. They held their hands up, trying to shield themselves from the spray.

Mary emerged from the trees, handling the heavy box. Jack and Max rushed over to help her.

"We can use my raft," she said, nodding to a blue raft nearby.

They carried the box toward the bank and lifted it into the front of the boat. Mary and Callie climbed in next to it. Jack took a seat in the middle. Max pushed the raft into the river and grabbed an oar from inside. After a few strokes, the foursome took off, leaving Mary's camp behind.

Chapter 7
The Ambush

As they rafted downstream, Jack soaked in the scenery. This part of California was absolutely beautiful. In addition to the green trees that lined both sides of the river, large gray boulders dotted the landscape.

"Do you know why the American River is so cold?" asked Mary.

Jack didn't think it was the air temperature. After all, it was hot outside.

"It comes from the snowmelt in the Sierra Nevada Mountains," she explained. "Before it gets here, the water has traveled nearly fifty miles."

Through the trees, Jack spied a squirrel scurrying on the ground with a nut in his mouth. Ahead, there was an extremely tall pine tree. It was at least four stories high.

"There's a bald eagle on top of that one," said Mary, pointing to the tree. "It's hunting for fish."

Jack knew that bald eagles were "fish eagles," but he could never understand why they were called "bald." After all, their head was covered in white feathers. Just as Jack was going to ask Mary that very question, Callie started to bark.

Woof!

Woof!

Woof!

But this time her barks weren't playful.

They sounded angry and frightened.
Callie's body was stiff, and the fur on her
back and tail was up. She was pointing at
something somewhere in the distance.

"It's okay," said Mary, stroking her fur.

"What do you think it is?" asked Max.

"Probably a bear," said Mary. "There are quite a few in these parts."

Jack didn't know about Max, but he

wasn't looking forward to running into a bear.

As the river turned right, Callie's barking only got worse. Not only was she woofing, she was also starting to growl.

Jack scanned the banks, looking for the signs of a dangerous animal. But aside from the harmless squirrels he had seen, there were no other animals in sight.

Then he spied something strange ahead. Standing on top of a large boulder to the side of the river were two skinny, bearded men.

One had red hair. The other's hair was white. The men were wearing tattered jeans and dirty short-sleeve shirts. Except for the fact that they had different colored beards, they looked the same. In fact, they were identical twins. They were also carefully watching the boat.

Jack wasn't sure what the men were up to, but he didn't like the look of them. Neither did Callie. Jack was about to warn the others when the men leaned down to touch their toes.

As the raft approached the boulder, they yanked a rope that was lying across their feet. It caught the front end of the boat and violently lifted it up and out of the water.

One by one, Jack, Max, Mary, Callie, and the strongbox tumbled out of the raft and into the river below.

Chapter 8
The Diversion

Jack couldn't believe it. They'd been ambushed!

But why?

The foursome had done nothing to the men. They didn't even know them.

Unfortunately for Jack, there was no time to think about those guys. The river had quickly pinned him against a boulder. The water was pushing on his chest, making it impossible for him to escape.

Behind him, he could hear Mary crying out.

"Callie!" she called.

Callie was paddling as hard as she could, but her head kept dipping under the water. Mary was trying to reach her, but her dog was on the opposite side of the river.

Just then, a blue blur sailed past Jack. Max was behind the raft, trying to swim after it. But without anyone in it, the raft was floating faster than anyone could

catch it. It quickly sped ahead of Max and
out of his reach.

SPLASH!

The sound came from the left bank.

The two men from the boulder bounded
into the river. Step by step, they began
to cross it, using the rope as a guide.
Midway through, they put their hands into
the water and pulled something out.

It was the strongbox!

The men began to hoot and holler.

"There's gold in them thar hills!" squealed the red-haired man.

"There's millions in it!" hollered the other.

They carried the strongbox across the river. As soon as they hit the right bank, they cut the rope and disappeared into the trees. Jack made a mental note of a yellow-leafed tree standing near the exit point.

If there was any question as to why the men had overturned their raft, it was now answered. Like the 49ers before them, the two greedy men were thirsty for gold.

Chapter 9
The Portable Rescue

Jack was furious. He had to tell the others.

But his position against the boulder was making it difficult for him to move. Jack stuck his feet down into the river and felt another large rock underneath. He stepped on it and pushed up as hard as he could. Then he thrust his body to the right. The river caught him and released him from the boulder.

The current swept him downstream.
Up ahead, there was a fallen log in the
river. Max and Mary had managed to grab
on to it. They climbed over its trunk and
headed for shore. Jack decided to do the
same.

As soon as he was near it, he seized
one of the branches and pulled himself

toward the log. Then he clambered on
top of the trunk and made his way to
Max and Mary on the bank. Unfortunately,
Callie was nowhere to be found. Mary
was initially furious.

"What were those guys *thinking*?" said
Mary. "That prank could have gotten us
killed!"

Then anger turned to sadness. Tears started to well up in Mary's eyes.

"And now," she said, "Callie is lost somewhere on the river."

Jack didn't think it was the time to tell Mary about the treasure. Besides, he and his brother might still be able to find it.

"Why don't Max and I retrieve the strongbox," offered Jack, "while you go after Callie."

"It'll be impossible," said Mary, "without a boat."

The river was too dangerous to swim. It was also moving faster than her feet would take her.

"I have an idea," said Max.

He pulled the GPF Kayak out of his bag. The GPF Kayak was the world's smallest portable kayak. Max opened the square pack, and the boat unfolded like an accordion. He put a couple of waterproof seals on its edges. Then he pulled a thin, short tube out of his bag. He yanked on the ends three times and the length of it tripled. Max uncapped the two ends, and an oval piece of plastic unfurled from each. This was the oar.

"Ta-da," said Max, handing it to Mary.

"You're incredible," she said.

If Max could get some compliments, reasoned Jack, so could he.

He noticed a bit of blood on Mary's arm. Guessing she'd cut herself on a rock, he ripped a piece of fabric from his shirt and wrapped it around the wound.

"You're amazing too," said Mary.

Jack blushed.

The boys helped Mary carry the kayak to the river. Once she was inside, they pushed her into the flow of the water.

"Good luck finding Callie!" shouted Jack as he waved.

Mary waved back and disappeared around the bend.

Chapter 10
The Hook

Jack and Max were now free to go after the box. Jack told his brother about the men. Until now, Max had no idea that the treasure had been stolen.

"But how did they know we were coming?" asked Max. "How did they even know that we were carrying gold?"

Jack shook his head. "No clue," he said.

There was no time to debate the

possibilities. At least twenty minutes had passed since Jack had seen the men walk off with the strongbox. They were at least a mile away from the yellow-leafed tree.

"We need to retrace our steps," said Max. "It we find the spot where they exited, we might be able to track them down."

The brothers hiked the mile upriver until Jack spotted the tree.

"That's where they escaped," said Jack, pointing to it and a narrow dirt path nearby.

The problem was that the boys were on the wrong side of the river. The rope that the men had used to get across had been cut in two.

"What about our grappling hooks?" asked Jack.

"Good idea," said Max.

Normally, the boys used these hooks to scale vertical walls. But here, they could use them as anchor points to pull themselves across the river.

The GPF's Grappling Hook looked like a jump rope, only there was a super strong nylon rope in between the two tubes.

Jack and Max pulled their Grappling Hooks out of their Book Bags and pushed a button on one of the tubes. A three-pronged hook popped out. They held on

to the other handle and threw the barbed
end as far as they could over the water.

Both hooks caught on a tree branch.
Jack and Max yanked on the rope to make
sure it was secure, then they held on to it
as they crossed the river.

When they got to the other side, they
retracted the barbs and tucked their
Grappling Hooks away. Jack and Max set off
on the dirt path in search of the thieves.

Chapter 11

The Abandoned Town

The boys hiked ten minutes through the
tall grasses that surrounded the dirt path.
Eventually, the grasses disappeared,
and the trail opened up into a small
abandoned town. The boys knew it was
abandoned because there was no one
living there.

"They probably left when the gold ran
out," said Max.

Through the middle of the town was a wide dirt road with four wooden buildings on either side. Some of the wooden planks went up and down, while others ran side to side. Most of the paint on the buildings had chipped off, and the windows were either cracked or missing. Some of the buildings didn't have doors.

On the right side of the road were the saloon, hardware store, general store, and blacksmith. To the left was the El Dorado Hotel, feed and tackle store, town jail, and a store with Chinese letters on it.

Since the town was quiet, Jack and Max could hear everything. They could hear the sound of the dirt swishing around in mini tornadoes on the road. They could hear the noise of signs creaking on iron chains. They could also hear the distinct sound of two men talking inside the saloon.

"I bet that's them," said Jack.

Jack and Max headed for it. They separated as they got to the swinging doors. Jack put his back up against the wall on the right, while Max took the left.

Because there was an opening at the top and bottom of the entrance, they could hear what was going on inside. But since it was difficult to see, Jack pulled out his Spy Scope.

The GPF Spy Scope was a black wire with a hidden camera on top. Once an agent synced the camera with his or her Watch Phone, he or she could spy on a criminal anytime and anywhere. The narrow, bendable wire could fit through holes, around corners, or through walls.

Jack bent the top of the Spy Scope upward and stuck it just under the saloon doors. A visual popped up on Jack's Watch Phone screen.

Inside, there were a couple of wooden tables and chairs. On the wall behind the bar at the back was a stained mirror. Sitting on one of the tables was the strongbox. The two men from the river were talking to each other.

Jack zoomed in to get a better look at the crooks. The man with the red hair was missing a couple of front teeth. Embroidered on the pocket of his shirt was the name "Lenny."

His twin with the white hair had all of his teeth, but he also had a large wart on the tip of his nose. His shirt pocket had the name "Benny."

"That dog sure shut up when it fell in the water!" said Benny.

"They didn't even know what hit 'em!" said Lenny. Lenny pulled something from his pocket and thrust it into the air. "And it's all thanks to this *bug*!"

In the palm of his right hand was a small clear box with an insect inside. As soon as Jack saw it, he realized this was no ordinary bug. It was a miniaturized drone built to look like a fly.

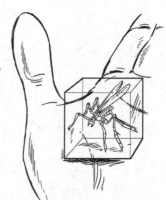

Just then, Jack remembered talking to Mary at the pit. A fly had been buzzing around his ear.

That same fly appeared again as he was standing near the river.

The reason why Lenny and Benny knew about the gold was now obvious. The men had been using the miniature drone to spy on Mary and her camp the entire time.

"When does the boss arrive?" asked Lenny.

Jack and Max looked at each other. There was a third man involved.

Benny looked at his watch.

"Any minute," he said.

Jack and Max didn't want to be noticed by the "boss." They quickly packed away the Spy Scope and dove down an alley to the left of the saloon. They hid behind a couple of wooden crates and patiently waited for the other man.

Chapter 12
The Boss

Although they couldn't see him yet, they could hear the "boss" coming.

CLIP.

CLOP.

CLIP.

CLOP.

The man strode by the alley and came into view.

He was riding a large brown horse with a white blaze on its nose. Behind the

69

horse was a flat wooden cart on wheels. The top of the cart was empty.

On the man's feet were red leather boots. Sitting on his head was a brown suede hat. The boys couldn't see the boss's face because the brim of his hat was casting a dark shadow. But they could tell he was bad news. There was a gun in the holster on his left hip and a knife in a sheath on his right.

The man pulled on the horse's reigns and came to a stop in front of the saloon. He swung his leg over the horse's back end and stepped down onto the ground. He faced the saloon and tipped his head forward. Then the man took off his hat.

Pulling a red bandanna from his back pocket, he wiped some sweat from his brow.

When he did, Jack noticed something

strange. The man was missing an
eyebrow above his right eye.

As soon as Jack saw that, Jack's heart
started to pound. His breathing grew
shallow. Sweat started to pool in the
palms of his hands.

"Are you okay?" whispered Max,
noticing Jack's strange behavior.

Jack shook his head. He wasn't all right.
He was having a panic attack. The odds

of this happening to him were supposed to be next to none.

Jack took a deep breath and tried to compose himself. As soon as the man walked inside, he leaned over to Max.

"That's Callous Carl," he said. "The world's most dangerous treasure hunter is back."

Chapter 13
The Bouncing Tooth

Max's eyes bugged out.

"Callous Carl?" said Max. "What's he doing in California?" asked Max.

That was a no-brainer as far as Jack was concerned. The man would do anything to get his calloused hands on a treasure. What Max was really asking was how he'd managed to get there so quickly from Mexico.

"Maybe he flew," said Jack. "Or he and his driver drove all night."

After all, the prison was only an eighteen-hour drive from northern California.

Either way, it didn't matter. Jack figured the wooden cart was brought in order to take the strongbox away.

"We need to stop him," said Max.

The boys came up with a plan. Jack decided to use the GPF's Gun Clamp to disable Callous's gun, while Max was going to use the Tornado to catch the three men.

The Stalwarts made their way back to the front of the saloon. But as Jack stepped onto the front porch, one of the wooden planks creaked. The sound echoed through the hollow town.

BANG!

A shot rang out from inside the saloon. A bullet flew through the opening above the doors and hit one of the buildings across the street. It narrowly missed the horse, causing it to rear its fore legs and neigh in fright. Jack dove into the alleyway to the right, while Max dove left.

Carl, Lenny, and Benny rushed from the saloon and onto the front porch. The swinging doors of the saloon flapped on their hinges behind them.

"Who's there?" barked Callous.

His eyes squinted, as he tried to find the source of the sound.

"Maybe it was the wind," said Lenny.

"Wind don't walk," said Callous. He lifted his noise into the air. "Smells like we got company."

He turned to the twins.

"I'll load the strongbox onto the cart," he scowled. "You two hunt the intruder down."

Jack hurried to the back of the saloon and hung a left. Then he peered down the alley where Max was supposed to be. But he was no longer there.

"You take that alleyway," said Benny, pointing to the place Jack had just come from. "I'll take this one."

With the twins closing in, Jack had no choice. He made a break for it.

He ran from the back of the saloon toward the back of the hardware store.

"There he is!" shouted Benny, spotting him at the end of the alley.

Jack went left and sprinted up alongside the hardware store. Ahead was an open window. He crawled through it and into the shop. Surrounding him was an extremely dusty space with lots of empty shelves.

"He's probably in the store!" called Benny to his brother. "You take the front!"

Jack was in trouble. He had to think fast. Lenny and Benny were planning to come at Jack from two sides. Leaning against the front door was a shovel. Jack grabbed it and laid the blade on the floor in front of the door.

Lenny burst into the shop and stepped on the shovel. Its wooden handle shot up and smacked him square in the face.

"Yowww!" hollered Lenny as one of his

remaining front teeth popped out onto
the floor.

Lenny ran after it, trying to catch it as it
bounced. It tumbled a few inches before
disappearing into a hole between two
floorboards.

"My tooth!" squealed Lenny. He got
down on his hands and knees and put his
eye to the hole.

Benny's head popped through the
window. When he saw his brother looking
for his tooth, he grew angry.

"Lenny'll never be able to say his 'th' words now!" said Benny, disappearing from view.

Jack sprinted through the front door. He quickly looked for any sign of Max in the road. But Max was nowhere to be found. Jack headed for the El Dorado Hotel across the street.

Suddenly, something grabbed Jack's Book Bag from behind. It was Benny. Benny yanked it off, causing Jack to nearly lose his balance. He regained his footing and carried on toward the hotel. Annoyed, Benny threw Jack's Book Bag down to the ground.

"Come here, you little brat!" he shouted.

Jack dashed through the hotel entrance. In front of him was a small, open area. There were a couple of dingy sofas with a coffee table in between them. Behind the sofas was a counter. To the right of the counter was a wall and farther to the right of that was a flight of stairs.

Jack quickly looked around. Max wasn't in here either. In fact, it looked like no one had been in the hotel for a hundred years. He dove behind the counter and hid. Benny entered seconds after Jack.

"I know you're in here," said Benny. "I ought to whack *you* in the mouth with a shovel."

Built into the backside of the counter were a collection of shelves. Jack looked in them to see if there was anything he could use. Unfortunately for Jack, all he could find was dust.

But then, Jack spied a painting hanging on the wall behind the counter. It was a portrait of a woman with curly black hair wearing a dress. There was a gold placard underneath with the name "Betty Lou House."

Jack reached up and yanked "Betty Lou" off the wall. As soon as Benny reached over the counter for him, he leaped up and smashed the painting over his head. The canvas ripped open. Benny's head popped out from underneath.

"Youch," said Benny, looking confused. Jack wedged the frame around the man's shoulders and dashed from the hotel.

But as soon as he got outside, Jack's body bounced off of something and onto the ground. He skidded on his backside for several feet. When Jack looked up to see what it was, he gasped.

It was Callous Carl.

"Looking for somethin'?" growled Callous.

To the man's right was Max. His wrists were tied together, and his Book Bag was missing. Jack could see it lying on the

wooden cart across the way. Callous's red bandanna was twisted and pulled tight across his mouth. Although Max didn't look injured, Jack was horrified.

Max tried to run, but Callous had him in a viselike grip. His hand was squeezing Max's arm so hard that there was no way he could get away.

Lenny was now standing in the road behind Callous, near where Jack's Book Bag was. He picked up Jack's gadget bag and tossed it onto the cart next to Max's Book Bag and the strongbox.

Callous bent down to Jack and looked him in square the eye. For a moment, Jack was relieved. Callous didn't seem to recognize him. But then something flickered in the man's eyes, and his expression turned from frustration to fury.

"You're that kid from Mexico!" he shouted. "The one that sent me to prison!"

He tossed Max to the ground like a rag doll. He called over to Lenny.

"Take care of him," Callous barked.

Callous reached down and grabbed Jack's shirt by the throat.

"While I take care of *you*," he said.

Chapter 14
The Surprise

Max tried to run for Jack. But Lenny jumped on him and pinned Max to the ground.

"Just like wrestling a gator!" squealed Lenny.

Callous lifted Jack high up in the air. Jack tried to throw a punch. But he missed. Jack kicked Callous in the gut. But instead of hurting the man, his foot only bounced off.

Callous laughed.

Carl carried Jack toward a building up ahead. The name on it said "Town Jail." Callous opened the door and stepped inside. Then he let the door shut behind them.

"That way," he said, grinning, "you and I can have a little privacy."

Callous's eyes scanned the room.

There was a broken wooden desk with three legs to the right. The only thing left of the cells were some iron bars lying on the floor.

Carl grunted. He wasn't pleased. But then he spied something against a wall. It was a couple of iron cuffs on chains.

"That'll do," said Callous.

He tossed Jack against the wall and quickly shackled him. Jack yanked his arms, trying to pull the chains out of the wall. But that didn't work. Callous picked up one of the broken iron bars from the floor.

"I've been dreaming about this for months," he said as he approached Jack. "Fate has brought you and me together again for a reason."

Carl lifted the bar over his head. Somewhere outside in the distance, Jack could hear something familiar. The sound was coming closer. Callous's crazed eyes glared at Jack.

"This is the last time," he said, "that you're going to come between me and my treasure."

"Any last words?" asked Callous as he lifted the iron bar even higher.

Jack didn't speak. He curled himself into a ball. Callous swung the bar downward.

BLAM!

The door to the jailhouse slammed to the floor. Something flew into the room.

Woof!
Woof!
Woof!
"What the—" said Callous, turning around.

Callie leaped up at Callous, sinking her teeth into his arm.

"Owww!" he howled in pain, letting go of the bar. It fell to the floor.

"Let go of me, you dumb dog!" shouted Callous as he tried to shake his arm free.

But Callie wasn't letting go.

Thinking quickly, Jack slipped his fingers under the cuff on his left wrist. He reached for his Melting Ink Pen at the side of his Watch Phone. He rubbed it against the cuff and watched as the inky chemical quickly ate through the iron. With one wrist free, he used it to free his other hand.

Jack had to find Max. Last he knew, Lenny was going to "take care of him."

"Callie, come!" said Jack.

The dog let go of Callous's arm and sprinted out of the jailhouse with Jack. The two of them raced toward the saloon.

Boiling in anger, Callous followed. He called to his men.

"Get after them!" he shouted.

Lenny and Benny came out of the saloon. When they saw Jack, they started to chase him too.

Jack raced past the cart and swiped his Book Bag. He put his thumb on the zip and popped it open. Reaching inside, he pulled out the GPF's Net Tosser. He hadn't used this device since his mission to China. But it was a perfect device for catching greedy gold hunters.

Jack looked over his shoulder. Callous, Lenny, and Benny were running side by side. He stopped in his tracks and turned to face the men.

"Your days of hunting treasure are over!" he shouted, as he tossed the ring into the air as far as he could. It hovered over the men until its position was just right.

Then it burst open, casting a wide net. The net fell to the ground, trapping Callous Carl, Lenny, and Benny inside.

"It's like a giant octopus!" hollered Lenny.

"Get us out of this thing!" shouted Callous, yanking on the rope.

But the Net Tosser was inescapable. The sides were permanently stuck to the ground.

That didn't stop Carl from trying. He pulled out his knife and tried to slice through the ropes. Little did he know, the GPF had made them with a special fiber that was yank-proof, cut-proof, and fireproof. Callous fired off a shot with his gun, but the bullet only ricocheted around inside. It bounced off the sides of the net, nearly hitting his men.

"Are you trying to get us *killed*!" said Benny.

Eventually, the bullet plugged itself into the dirt.

After twenty minutes, the men gave up trying. They grumpily plonked themselves on the ground in the road. Jack asked Callie to stand guard.

"Sit," he said.

Callie dutifully sat in front of the net.
Every time the men moved, she growled
at them, flashing them her pointed
white teeth.

Chapter 15
The Nose Knows

With the criminals now under control, Jack
set about trying to find Max. His first stop
was the saloon.

Sure enough, Max was there. Lenny
had tied Max to one of the chairs. Jack
opened the heel of Max's left boot and
pulled out his pocketknife. He used it to
set Max free.

"Thanks," said Max, rubbing his sore
wrists.

Together, the boys made their way outside.

Walking toward them was a familiar face. It was Mary.

"There you are!" she said. "Callie and I were looking all over for you. She ran ahead. It's taken me a while to catch up!"

Just then, Mary noticed Callie. Her dog was sitting in the middle of the road, glaring at some frustrated-looking men under a net. She recognized Lenny and Benny.

"Are those the guys from the river?" she said. "What are they doing here?"

The boys told her what had happened. They explained how the men had tried to steal the gold. Like Callie, she narrowed her eyes at the men.

"It looks like they got what they deserved," she said. "Did you manage to recover the treasure?"

Jack and Max escorted her to the
flat wooden cart. On top of it was the
strongbox. Mary opened the lid. She
surveyed the contents inside.

"Everything seems to be here," she said.
"Without the two of you," she added,
"that might not have been the case."

"How did you and Callie find us?"
asked Max. After all, the last time they'd
seen Mary, she was a few hundred yards
downriver on the opposite side.

"You're not going to believe this," said Mary. "But after I found Callie, we hiked back to the spot where the boat tipped over."

Mary directed her next comments to Jack.

"I let her sniff the fabric that you gave me to cover my cut," she said. "She smelled it and tracked your scent."

Jack couldn't believe it. He already knew Callie was an amazing dog. But to have tracked him all this way meant that she had a very special skill indeed. He walked over to her and knelt down, so that his face was in front of her hers. He looked Callie in the eye.

"You're incredible," he said, giving her a kiss.

Callie gave Jack a kiss too. All over his face.

Chapter 16
The Farewell

Jack used his Watch Phone to contact
the local authorities. Within the hour, the
Placer County police had arrived. Jack
released the ropes to the Net Tosser using
his Watch Phone. They scooped the men
up off the ground, cuffed them, and then
dragged them to a waiting helicopter.

"Can we call our momma?" said Benny.
"I need to tell her we won't be home for
dinner."

As they boarded the helicopter, Callous Carl looked down at Jack. He snarled and curled his upper lip. But this time, the man didn't intimidate Jack. The "world's most dangerous treasure hunter" was no longer. Jack had managed to beat him . . . twice. The man was now going to a maximum security prison where there was absolutely no chance of escape.

As soon as the men were inside, the helicopter door closed. The chopper took off.

Mary and Callie came to say good-bye.

"The police are taking us and the strongbox to the next town," said Mary.

Mary hugged the boys, like a mother would hug her sons.

"I'm so proud of the two of you," she said. "Thanks again for everything that you did."

"We're happy we could help," said Jack.

He bent down to Callie. She gave him
her paw. He shook it.

"I'm going to miss you," he told Callie.
Jack could feel the sting of tears forming
in his eyes. "You saved my life."

"We'll keep in touch," said Mary.

One of the male police officers
interrupted them.

"We're ready for you, ma'am," he said
as he gently placed his hand on her back.

Mary and Callie followed the policeman to a second chopper. Two other policemen lifted the strongbox into the craft. After helping Mary and Callie inside, they closed the door behind them.

Jack and Max could see Mary and Callie sitting together inside. The Stalwart brothers waved to them. Then Mary, Callie, and the strongbox disappeared into the sky.

Chapter 17
The New Recruit

After using their GPF's Portable Maps,
Jack and Max returned home to England.
Over the next several days, they rested.
They weren't called on any missions, so
they got to do what ordinary kids did at
night. They worked on their homework,
played games with their family, and
read books.

One day after school, Jack came home
to find an envelope lying on his desk. The

outside made it look like a letter from a "Book of the Month" club. The return address was "Great Picks for Fiver," or GPF. This clever trick was how the GPF sent snail mail letters to its agents without their parents finding out.

Jack ripped open the envelope. Inside was a photograph of Callie.

She was sitting proudly, wearing a gold medal draped around her shoulders. Standing next to her was Mary. Jack flipped the photo over. There was a handwritten message on the other side.

Dear Jack,

Thought you'd like to see the GPF's latest recruit! Because of Callie's extraordinary work in saving you, the GPF recently awarded her with its highest honor—the "Gold Medal of Bravery." Can you believe it? They've also asked her to become a K-9 agent. Doesn't she look proud of herself?

Callie will continue to live and travel with me, but whenever the GPF needs her, she'll be reporting for duty. Hopefully, the two of you will be able to work again together soon.

Lots of love,
Mary and Callie

P.S. Thanks again for everything that you and Max did to save the strongbox. The contents have now been authenticated and are on their way to the 1849 Museum in San Francisco, California. This way, children can learn more about the California Gold Rush.

Jack looked at the photo of Callie and smiled. He was so proud of her. There were only ten dogs in the world worthy of being chosen for the GPF K-9 unit. Jack only wished he'd been there for the ceremony to shake her paw.

Although he wanted to post Callie's photo on his pegboard, he couldn't. His parents had no idea that he and Max were secret agents for the GPF. This photo was going to have to remain top secret too.

Jack walked over to his bookshelf and pulled out his American history book. This was one of his several Diversion Safes. Jack opened it up to the hollowed out center. Already inside were a few of his mementos.

The necklace from Chief Abasi in Kenya was there, as was the fake press pass from his adventure in Italy. The coded note from Max was in there too. This was the letter that Jack used to figure out where Max was in Egypt. Jack placed Callie's photo on the top of the stack.

He looked one last time at her smiling face.

"Hope to see you again soon," he said.

Then Jack closed the book and placed it back on the shelf.

See where the
adventure began...

Book 1:
The Escape of the
Deadly Dinosaur
(New York City, USA)

Book 2:
The Search for the
Sunken Treasure
(Australia)

Book 3:
The Mystery of
the Mona Lisa
(France)

Book 4:
The Caper of the
Crown Jewels
(England)

Book 5:
The Secret of the
Sacred Temple
(Cambodia)

Book 6:
The Pursuit of the
Ivory Poachers
(Kenya)

Book 7:
The Puzzle of the
Missing Panda
(China)

Book 8:
Peril at the
Grand Prix
(Italy)

Book 9:
The Deadly Race
to Space
(Russia)

Book 10:
The Quest for
Aztec Gold
(Mexico)

Book 11:
The Theft of the
Samurai Sword
(Japan)

Book 12:
The Fight for the
Frozen Land
(Arctic)